Rockets

A & C Black • London

Rockets

MR CROC - Frank Rodgers

What Mr Croc Forgot

Mr Croc's Clock

Mr Croc's Walk

Mr Croc's Silly Sock

First paperback edition 1999
First published 1999 in hardback by
A & C Black (Publishers) Ltd
35 Bedford Row, London WC1R 4JH

ISBN 0-7136-5048-6

A CIP catalogue record for this book is available from the British Library.

Printed and bound by G. Z. Printek, Bilbao, Spain.

Mr Croc woke up feeling very hungry. He'd been dreaming about food all night long... as usual.

He got
dressed and
hurried to
the kitchen.

There he ate his usual HUGE breakfast.

A bowl of
porridge...

...two glasses
of juice...

...another bowl
of porridge with
doughnuts on top...

...toast and jam,
toast and honey,
toast and
bananas...

...toast and
sardines...

...a plateful of
fishfingers...

...and four
cups of tea.

As soon as breakfast was over, Mr Croc began to think about his dinner.
'I will go shopping straight away,' he said.

Mr Croc liked fish.

He tied a bit of string round one of his fingers so he wouldn't forget.

Mr Croc was very forgetful.

Only the day before he had forgotten to get dressed...

...and walked down the street in his pyjamas!

Before he set off for the shops, Mr Croc brushed his teeth. This took a long time. Mr Croc had one hundred teeth.

And he was proud of every one.

He thought he had the loveliest smile in the world.

At last he was ready to go. As he walked down the street, he smiled and said hello to everyone he met.

Mr Croc has such a lovely smile!

Outside the grocer's shop he met his friend, Mr Hound.

'Hello Mr Croc,' said Mr Hound.

'To remind me to buy something,' said Mr Croc. 'But I can't remember what.'

They looked in the grocer's window.
It was full of pies, flans, eggy things
and cheesy things.

They went into the grocer's. Mr Croc bought twenty tasty cheesy things from Mrs Deli, the grocer.

He was so busy making sure that she noticed all his one hundred teeth, that he nearly walked into the door.

Mr Hound opened it just in time.

Off they went along the street until they came to the baker's shop.

The window was full of cakes, tarts, biscuits and buns.

Mr Croc looked
at the string on
his finger.
He looked
at the cheesy
things in
his bag.

'Perhaps it wasn't cheesy things that I meant to buy after all,' he said.

They went into the baker's shop. Mr Croc bought a big bag of cakes from Mr Crust, the baker.

As Mr Croc smiled his lovely smile, he caught sight of himself in the shop mirror.

He smiled even more... and nearly walked into a wedding cake.

Mr Hound pushed it aside just in time.

Off they went once more until they came to the sweet shop.

The window was full of crisps, toffees, lollipops, chocolate and lemonade.

Mr Croc looked at the string on his finger.

He looked at the cheesy things and cakes in his bag.

'Perhaps it wasn't cakes and cheesy things I meant to buy,' he said.

They went into the sweet shop.
Mr Croc bought a big bag of sweets, crisps and lemonade from Mrs Gum, the owner.

Mr Croc waved goodbye. To make sure Mrs Gum saw all the teeth in his lovely smile, he walked backwards out of the shop and nearly tripped over a crate of cola.

Mr Hound moved it just in time.

When they were safely out of the shop,
Mr Hound said goodbye.
'I have to do my own shopping now,'
he said.

Mr Croc set off *again*, until he came to the fish shop.

He looked in the window...

...and saw his reflection.

Just then,
Mrs Poodle
came out
of the shop
carrying two
shopping bags.

She was in
so much of
a hurry...

...and Mr Croc
was so busy
admiring
himself that...

...they walked into each other.

Mrs Poodle
dropped one
of her bags.
It rolled
off the
pavement...

...into the road...

...and under a bus.

The bus ran over the bag and squashed everything flat.

Mrs Poodle looked at the sticky mess and began to cry.

‘Oh dear,’ said Mr Croc. ‘I am sorry, Mrs Poodle.’

Mrs Poodle blew her nose.

‘It’s not your fault, Mr Croc,’ she sniffed. ‘But that bag had all the food for my son’s birthday party in it.’

She held up her other bag. 'All I've got left is this fish that I bought for my supper,' she wailed.

Mrs Poodle began to cry again.

Mr Croc looked at the string on his finger.

He shouted so loudly that Mrs Poodle stopped crying.

‘Fish!’ cried Mr Croc.

Suddenly Mr Croc had an idea.

'What sort of things did you buy for your son's party, Mrs Poodle?' he asked.

And lemonade?
Of course...
And cheesy things?
Well yes... I did buy some tasty cheesy things.

'Mrs Poodle!' laughed Mr Croc. 'Guess what I've got in my bag?'

'What?' asked Mrs Poodle.

'You see,' he said, 'I tied string round my finger to remind me to buy fish but instead I bought...'

'Exactly,' said Mr Croc.

'But you must,' said Mr Croc.

He smiled his lovely smile.

Then Mrs Poodle had an idea. She held up her shopping bag. 'Why don't we swap?' she said.

So they swapped shopping.

Now... there's one more thing you must do, Mr Croc.
What's that?
You must come to the party, of course.
BRILLIANT!

Mr Croc had a wonderful time at the party. He played hide and seek...

...pass the parcel...

...and when the record player broke down he played the piano for musical chairs.

Everyone was glad he came.

Then it was time to eat. The children ate the party food...

...and Mr Croc made a big plate of fish and chips for himself and Mrs Poodle.

'This is the best party I've ever been to,' said Mr Croc.

Everyone agreed.

Mr Croc smiled a HUGE smile...

...showing every one of his one hundred, lovely teeth.

The End